BOTH AND NEITHER
My Intersex Life
Part 1
By Malcom Adrian Highgate

WARNING: OVER 18 ONLY
This book contains explicit sexual content and themes that are intended for mature audiences only. It is not suitable for readers under the age of 18. Reader discretion is advised.
All Characters and events in this publication, other than those clearly in the public domain, are fictitious and any resemblance to real persons, alive or dead is purely coincidental.

Copyright 2024 © Malcom Adrian Highgate.
All rights reserved including the moral right. No part of this publication may be reproduced, stored in a retrieval system, or transmitted in any form or by any means, without the prior written permission in writing of the author, nor be otherwise circulated in any form of binding or cover other than that in which the author intended and without a similar condition including this condition being imposed on the subsequent purchaser.

Chapter 1. Becoming Isabella

Hi. My name is Isabella Del Rio. I'm an American Brazilian intersex person, 24 years of age, and if there's one thing, I've learned in my short but eventful life, it's that identity is never as simple as it seems. I stand at 5 feet 10 inches, with long, jet-black hair that falls down my back in a straight, silky cascade, and baby-blue eyes that catch the light in a way that always seems to draw attention. People often say I look like I belong on a runway, but what they don't see—what they never suspect—is the complexity that lies beneath the surface.

Growing up in New York, surrounded by a world that loved its labels and tidy boxes, I had to learn to navigate spaces that weren't made for people like me. I was born with both a normal, functioning vagina and a 10-inch penis, a reality that made my existence feel like a battleground long before I understood what it meant to be intersex. But my story isn't just about anatomy; it's about learning to embrace every part of who I am, to rise in a world that rarely knows how to handle difference.

At 24, I've already faced more challenges than some people do in a lifetime, but I've also built a life I'm proud of. I'm a lawyer at one of the top corporate firms in New York City, carving out my path in the high-stakes world of finance, tech, construction, and pharmaceuticals. My days are a whirlwind of boardroom negotiations and legal strategy sessions, and my nights—well, let's just say they're full of a different kind of adventure.

But we'll get to that. For now, let's start at the beginning. Because every story, no matter how complicated, has one.

Ohh......and I have a 10-inch penis and a beautifully shaped vagina, and I am very proud of both.

Sometimes, I look back at my childhood in Scarsdale, and it feels like a dream wrapped in layers of warmth and complexity. Our elegant but unpretentious colonial home sat on a tree-lined street in Westchester County, surrounded by picturesque parks and neighbors who seemed as driven as they were wealthy. The house had white columns that seemed to reach for the sky, a perfectly manicured lawn, and bay windows that let in beams of sunlight that danced across the hardwood floors. It was a place full of laughter, debates, and a family that was, in many ways, the epitome of middle-class success.

Dad, George, was the backbone of our stability. An accountant who worked tirelessly in Manhattan, he was as meticulous with numbers as he was with the way he approached our family's well-being. Even though his days were filled with tax codes and balance sheets, he always made time for us, especially on Fridays when he'd take us out for ice cream. He was reserved, a man of order, but his love for us was woven into every small, thoughtful thing he did.

Then there was Mom, Elizabeth, a structural engineer who shattered glass ceilings with quiet grace. I used to watch her sketch blueprints late into the night, her hands moving with a kind of fluid precision that made me marvel at her brilliance. Mom was my role model, a figure of strength and intellect. Yet even she struggled to map out a clear path through the labyrinth of my identity. How could she design skyscrapers that defied gravity but not know how to guide me through my own complexities?

Emily and Marcus, my older siblings, carved out their places in our world. Emily, the golden child, could have probably played the piano in Carnegie Hall if she wanted to. Her fingers danced across the keys, filling the house with music that was as perfect as her GPA. Yet for all her achievements, she had a heart of gold. She was my second mother in many ways, always ready to pick me up when life pushed me down, even if she couldn't fully understand my struggles.

Marcus, my carefree brother, was my protector. He was the life of any party, the soccer star who made friends easily, but he never hesitated to defend me when things got tough. Even as we grew older and his focus shifted to his teenage adventures, he always had a way of making me feel safe. I needed that protection because, even though I was loved at home, the world outside was far less forgiving.

Growing up intersex in a place like Scarsdale, where perfection seemed to be the norm, was a challenge that no child should have to face. My parents, faced with overwhelming decisions when I was born, chose to let me grow into my own identity rather than force me into a box. I'm grateful for that, but it came with its own set of complications. School was brutal. The children of doctors, lawyers, and hedge fund managers didn't take kindly to anyone different. My academic success and sharp mind were supposed to shield me, but they only made me more isolated.

The whispers began subtly, growing louder with every passing year. Bathrooms were war zones, and locker rooms were places of dread. If I dared to walk into the girls' locker room, the other girls would either glare or leave, their unease palpable. Trying to use the boys' locker room was even worse—jeers, snickers, and crude jokes that followed me through the halls. I became a master of avoidance, mapping out routes through the school that would minimize contact and keep me safe.

Rumors spread like wildfire. People made a game of mocking my "strangeness," reducing my identity to something ugly and unworthy. Marcus defended me when he could, but he was just a teenager himself, caught between protecting his little sister and navigating his own social life. Emily, by then away at college, called often and listened to me cry, but she was too far away to stop the daily torment.

The home was my sanctuary. The library, with its mahogany shelves and quiet corners, was where I discovered my love for the law. It was a place where I felt powerful and in control, where I imagined a world where justice and order were more than abstract concepts. My mother's architectural journals and my father's tax books were there, too, as if the room was a blend of everything that made our family both complicated and beautiful.

My childhood was a balancing act between comfort and complexity, love and pain. It's what shaped me, and made me resilient, and unafraid. But even now, as I write this, I can feel the echoes of that time—the confusion, the loneliness, and the small victories that kept me going.

The psychological toll of high school was something I wouldn't wish on anyone. I remember developing this ritual, this desperate attempt to protect myself: walking the perimeter of the school building during lunch. It was a way to avoid the cafeteria, a place where my classmates might corner me, where their cruelty took on new and more creative forms. They'd hurl insults, push my books out of my hands, and delight in making me feel small. I became an expert at hiding pain. Every night, I would practice my smile in the mirror until it was believable until it could convince Mom and Dad that I was fine. On the outside, I was perfect—top grades, praised by teachers—but inside, my mental health was unraveling.

The loneliness only grew as my body changed. Puberty was a nightmare that magnified everything that made me different. My intersex condition made every physical change feel like an assault, something I had to hide and be ashamed of. My body didn't fit into any of the neat, binary categories my peers expected, and that only made the ridicule sharper. Every day felt like a battlefield, and I was fighting a war with no end in sight.

The breaking point came during sophomore year. I'll never forget that day. A group of boys cornered me and tore into me with their words, mocking me in front of half the student body. They called me a "freak" and told me I didn't belong. Their laughter echoed in my mind long after the crowd had dispersed. I remember feeling shattered like all the strength I had been clinging to was gone.

That night, the weight of everything became too heavy to bear. I sat alone in my room, the house silent except for the hum of the dishwasher downstairs, and I wrote a note. I tried to explain to my family why I couldn't keep fighting and why the pain was too much. Tears streamed down my face, blurring the words, and I truly believed that this was the end.

But Marcus came home early from soccer practice. He must have sensed something was wrong because he knocked on my door, and when I didn't answer, he barged in. He found me in a moment I wish I could erase, and the look on his face will always haunt me. He held me as I sobbed, whispering that he wouldn't let me go, that he needed me here. That moment changed everything. My family rallied around me, shaken but determined to help me heal.

Therapy became my lifeline. It was a place where I could finally unravel everything: my identity, the trauma, the feeling that I would never be enough. Mom and Dad began to educate themselves, to understand what I had been going through. The road to recovery wasn't straightforward, and there were still plenty of dark days, but something shifted in me. The experience didn't break me; it made me stronger and more determined to face the world.

When I arrived at Yale, it felt like stepping into a new chapter, one I had fought so hard to reach. The sun was shining, and everything about the campus buzzed with possibility. It was the fresh start I had dreamed of. Moving into my dorm was surreal, a mix of excitement and nerves. My parents and Marcus helped me settle in, their pride almost palpable. Mom hugged me

tight, whispering, "You've come so far," and Marcus, ever the joker, told me to show everyone how it's done.

When they left, I stood in the quiet of my new room, taking it all in. This was my space, my chance to be whoever I wanted. No more hiding. No more fear.

Yale was a world away from the judgment of high school. Here, people came from every walk of life, carrying stories that were as complicated as mine. During my first week, I met Sofia, an art history major with an infectious laugh and a love for colorful scarves. We bonded over bad cafeteria food and classic literature. She was one of the first people I opened up to about my past, and for the first time in a long while, I felt seen.

Classes were intense, but I thrived on the challenge. Constitutional Law became my favorite, and I loved every moment spent debating landmark cases. But it wasn't always smooth. Sometimes, the weight of my past pressed down on me, the echoes of cruel laughter still haunting my nights. Therapy remained a crucial part of my routine, and I leaned on the strategies I had learned to keep moving forward.

Socially, Yale offered a fresh start, but navigating relationships was still tricky. I was careful about disclosing my intersex identity, never knowing how people would react. Yet, to my surprise, I found acceptance more often than not. The LGBTQ+ community at Yale became my refuge, a place where I could finally be unapologetically myself.

Then there was Ethan. We met at a queer students' mixer, and something about his green eyes and passion for human rights advocacy drew me in. We connected over our shared dreams of using the law to make a difference, and I found myself falling for his warmth and genuine interest in who I was. But I was cautious. Opening up was still a risk, and I wasn't sure if I was ready to let him see all of me.

The debate team became another outlet, a place where I could channel everything, I had been through into something powerful. My first major debate was on gender-based discrimination in the workplace, a topic that hit close to home. Standing at the podium, my voice unwavering, I poured my heart into my argument. Winning that debate felt like reclaiming a piece of myself.

Even with all the success, doubt sometimes crept in. The shadows of my past still lingered, but each day I reminded myself of how far I had come. My scars, visible and invisible, were no longer things to hide. They were a testament to my journey, to the strength I had found within myself. Yale was just the beginning, but it was a beginning I had earned, and I was ready to take on whatever came next.

The meeting sealed the deal. By the end of her final semester, I had accepted an offer from Whitaker, Hargrove & Crane, one that came with a highly competitive salary, a generous signing bonus, and a promise: I would be fast-tracked to work on major cases, something unheard of for new associates. Yet, the firm's expectations were sky-high, and I knew I had to be at my very best.

Before I could start my career, there was one last challenge: the New York State Bar Exam. The exam was infamous for its grueling nature, testing not just one's knowledge of the law but also the ability to perform under extreme pressure. For months, I buried myself in bar prep courses, filling her days with study sessions and practice tests. The weight of expectation loomed heavily over her, not just from the firm but also from herself. I had come so far, but this final hurdle was crucial. I couldn't let myself stumble.

When exam day arrived, I felt a mixture of anxiety and determination. I entered the exam hall in lower Manhattan, surrounded by hundreds of other aspiring lawyers, each one just as tense and focused as I was. For two days, I wrote and reasoned my way through questions about contracts, constitutional law, and criminal procedures, pouring everything I had into those blue books. As I walked out of the exam room on the final day, I was exhausted yet hopeful, a small flicker of pride already beginning to burn in her chest.

The wait for the bar exam results was agonizing, but I had learned patience and perseverance. I threw myself into the things I loved: dinners with friends, weekend hikes to clear her mind, and moments of quiet reflection in the library that had always felt like home. Finally, the results came in: I had passed, and not just by a small margin—her scores placed her among the top performers. It was a moment of triumph, a validation of everything I had fought for.

The first day at Whitaker, Hargrove & Crane was nothing short of exhilarating. I walked into the towering glass skyscraper in midtown Manhattan, dressed impeccably in a tailored navy-blue suit and carrying a sleek leather briefcase. The marble floors gleamed, and the air was thick with the energy of high-stakes legal battles and multimillion-dollar deals. The firm's lobby was a sea of well-dressed associates, partners, and clients, but I moved through it with confidence, her head held high.

Her role as a junior associate in the finance law division came with immediate responsibilities. Instead of spending her first weeks buried in menial tasks, I was placed on a team handling a massive corporate merger between two global banks—a case that would set the tone for her entire career. Under the mentorship of senior partner Amanda Liu, a formidable finance attorney known for her strategic brilliance and razor-sharp mind, I began learning the intricacies of high-stakes negotiations, corporate governance, and financial regulations.

The work was relentless. Twelve-hour days were the norm, and weekends were often spent reviewing documents and drafting briefs. But I thrived in the chaos. The office became her new battlefield, and I faced every challenge with the same resilience that had carried her through high school and Yale. I quickly earned a reputation for her meticulous attention to detail and her ability to think several moves ahead, an asset in a field where one mistake could cost millions of dollars.

Yet, even in the high-pressure world of corporate law, I remained true to myself. Her presence was as striking as her intellect, and I made no effort to hide who I was. Her colleagues, who came from all walks of life, admired her courage and authenticity. At times, whispers about her intersex identity made their way through the office grapevine, but I handled them with grace and dignity, addressing questions and curiosities with the same confidence I brought to the courtroom.

The fast-paced world of finance law brought its own set of rewards. I attended lavish client dinners in some of New York's finest restaurants and mingled with executives whose decisions moved markets. I found myself in rooms where the future of companies was decided, and her voice—young but powerful—was heard and respected. The journey had only just begun, but I knew that I was right where I was meant to be at the forefront of a field where her intellect, resilience, and identity all had a role to play.

With her career off to a blazing start, I knew that finding her own place in Manhattan was a necessary step toward independence and fully embracing the life I had always dreamed of. After weeks of searching and countless viewings, I finally settled on an apartment in the upscale neighborhood of **Tribeca**. The area, known for its cobblestone streets and historic warehouses converted into luxury lofts, was the perfect blend of sophistication and vibrancy.

Her new home was a one-bedroom apartment located on the 10th floor of a sleek, glass-fronted building that offered stunning views of the Hudson River. The building itself boasted a minimalist, modern design, complete with 24-hour concierge service, a state-of-the-art gym, and a rooftop terrace where residents could unwind with a glass of wine and watch the sunset over the city.

The apartment was everything I had envisioned: spacious yet cozy, with high ceilings and floor-to-ceiling windows that bathed the space in natural light. The open-concept living area featured polished hardwood floors and a neutral color palette of soft greys and whites, accented by touches of gold and navy. I carefully curated the decor to reflect my sophisticated yet warm personality. A plush velvet sofa in a rich navy hue sat in the center of the room, adorned with silk throw pillows and a cashmere blanket that invited me to sink in after a long day at the firm.

My bookshelves were a testament to my love of the law and literature, filled with thick law journals, classic novels, and a few beloved pieces of fiction that she had carried with me since my days in Scarsdale. A minimalist glass coffee table held a few scattered magazines and a decorative tray with candles, a nod to my love of creating a serene, welcoming atmosphere.

The kitchen, though compact, was impeccably designed with marble countertops, high-end stainless-steel appliances, and sleek white cabinetry. It was a space I cherished, even though she rarely had time to cook elaborate meals. Still, she enjoyed preparing me a quick breakfast of avocado toast and espresso in the mornings, savoring the quiet moments before the chaos of my workday began.

My bedroom was a sanctuary, painted in soft, calming hues of lavender and dove grey. The bed, dressed in Egyptian cotton sheets and a luxurious down comforter, was framed by a tufted headboard in light grey velvet. On my nightstand sat a simple lamp, a stack of books she was in the process of reading, and a small, framed photo of my family, a reminder of the people who had supported me through every challenge. A walk-in closet held my collection of tailored suits, designer heels, and the few statement pieces she loved to wear when she wanted to stand out.

The bathroom was equally luxurious, with a deep soaking tub and a glass-enclosed rainfall shower. Marble tiles covered the floors and walls, and the vanity was adorned with elegant brass fixtures. It was a space she used not just for getting ready but for unwinding, often soaking in the tub with a glass of wine and a book after particularly long days at Whitaker, Hargrove & Crane.

Despite my demanding schedule, I made time to personalize my apartment, adding touches that made it feel like home. She hung abstract artwork she had collected from local galleries and kept a vase of fresh flowers on the kitchen island, a small but meaningful indulgence. The space was both a reflection of my hard work and a testament to how far she had come—from a tormented teenager in Scarsdale to a successful, independent woman making my mark in New York.

Living in Tribeca also meant that I was never far from the pulse of the city. The neighborhood's upscale cafes, boutique shops, and art galleries provided the perfect escape when she needed a break from my high-pressure job. And yet, within the walls of my apartment, she found peace—a place where I could be myself, free from judgment and full of promise for the future.

I stood at 5 feet 10 inches tall, my presence commanding and elegant. My long, straight black hair cascaded down my back like a silky waterfall, contrasting beautifully with my flawless, porcelain skin. My hair framed a face that could easily grace the cover of a high-fashion magazine: high cheekbones, a well-defined jawline, and full, naturally pink lips that curved into an enigmatic smile. My baby blue eyes, vivid and almost ethereal, were my most captivating features, drawing people in with their piercing, magnetic gaze.

My body was a harmonious blend of feminine curves and striking, powerful features. My breasts, a full and natural C-cup, added to my soft and graceful silhouette, accentuated by a slender waist that flared into gently curving hips. My long legs, toned and shapely, seemed to go on forever, a result of years of discipline and an active lifestyle. They carried me with a graceful stride, exuding confidence whether I was strutting through a courtroom or commanding attention in a designer dress.

Yet, my anatomy held a complexity that made me uniquely myself. Alongside my normal, functioning vagina, I also had a 10-inch penis, a part of my intersex identity that I had come to embrace with pride and confidence. It was a part of me that had once caused me great turmoil, but I had since learned to see it as a source of my strength and individuality. My body was a testament to my journey, a blend of masculine and feminine that defied traditional definitions and celebrated my authenticity.

My hands, with long, elegant fingers that could have belonged to a concert pianist, moved gracefully whether I was flipping through legal documents or gesturing passionately during an argument. My nails were always perfectly manicured, adding to my polished and sophisticated appearance.

Everything about me radiated a sense of refined beauty and striking allure. My fashion-model facial features, combined with my statuesque frame, made me a head-turner wherever I went. But beyond my physical beauty lay a complexity and confidence that left a lasting impression on everyone I encountered. I was more than my anatomy, more than the sum of my striking features; I am a powerful, intelligent, and fiercely resilient woman who has embraced every part of myself.

My journey through love and relationships has been as complex and transformative as the rest of my life, filled with both joy and pain. My first experience with love was bittersweet, leaving scars that took years to heal. In high school, amidst the torment and confusion I faced, a bright spot emerged in the form of Ian, a charming senior with an infectious smile and an effortless confidence that made him irresistible to almost everyone. He was the first person I fell in love with, and I believed—naively, in retrospect—that he felt the same.

Ian made me feel seen in a way I had desperately craved. His touch, his laughter, and the way he whispered my name made my heart race and gave me a glimmer of hope in the otherwise harsh world of high school. I trusted him enough to share my deepest secret: my intersex condition. It was a leap of faith, one I took with a pounding heart and the desperate hope that love could make someone see me for who I truly was.

But Ian turned out to be far from the person I had hoped he would be. The next day, the entire school buzzed with the revelation he had cruelly shared. My condition became the subject of vicious gossip and ridicule, magnifying the bullying I had already endured. The betrayal cut deep, and the humiliation was crushing. It was this ultimate betrayal that led me to the brink, to that dark moment when I nearly ended my life. It took years to recover, and even longer to trust anyone with my heart again.

My next serious relationship came during my years at Yale. By then, I had become a stronger, more self-assured person. Enter Jonathan, a brilliant and open-minded mathematics student who approached the world with a sense of wonder and curiosity. Jonathan was the opposite of Ian: compassionate, understanding, and genuine. We met in a shared study group and bonded over our mutual love for logic and debate. He was fascinated by my legal mind, while I admired his ability to turn the abstract world of mathematics into something poetic.

Jonathan didn't see me as a curiosity or an anomaly. Instead, he saw me as a beautiful, multifaceted woman with a brilliant mind and a spirit that had survived more than most people could imagine. Our relationship was gentle, filled with nights spent laughing over bad takeout and days exploring Yale's historic campus together. I opened up to him about my past, and unlike Ian, Jonathan respected and cherished my trust. He supported my dreams and helped me heal some of the emotional wounds that still lingered.

But when graduation approached, reality set in. Jonathan had always dreamed of moving back to California to work at a prestigious tech company, while my future was firmly rooted in New York. We parted ways amicably, with tearful goodbyes and a promise to stay in touch. Our breakup was painful, but it was also mature and filled with mutual respect. Even now, we remain close friends, exchanging texts and calls whenever one of us needs a familiar voice to lean on.

After graduating and landing my position at Whitaker, Hargrove & Crane, my life became a whirlwind of career success. But amidst the late nights and high-stakes cases, I found myself drawn to Maria, a vibrant, fiercely independent woman with a shock of fiery red hair and a magnetic presence. Maria was American-Irish, raised in a devout Catholic family, and had a rebellious streak that made her irresistible. We met at a charity gala I attended as part of my firm's outreach, and sparks flew almost immediately.

Maria challenged me in ways no one else had. She was passionate, stubborn, and full of life, with a laugh that lit up any room. Our relationship was a beautiful escape from the stress of my professional world, filled with spontaneous weekend getaways, nights spent dancing in underground clubs, and lazy mornings cooking breakfast together in my Tribeca apartment. It was the kind of romance that made me feel alive, even if it was destined to be short-lived.

Despite our deep connection, Maria's traditional upbringing clashed with the reality of my identity. Maria struggled to reconcile her Catholic beliefs with the complexities of my intersex experience. We had countless heartfelt conversations, but the tension remained, an undercurrent that neither of us could ignore. Eventually, we parted ways, both heartbroken but understanding that love, no matter how beautiful, isn't always enough. Maria left an indelible mark on my heart, and though our time together was brief, it was filled with memories I will always cherish.

And then, there was nothing. Zilch. Nil. Zero. Since Maria, I have thrown myself into my work, using the long hours and intellectual challenges of finance law as a way to distract myself from the loneliness. My career demanded everything I had, and in many ways, it was easier to focus on my professional life than to risk my heart again. I had grown wary of the complexities that came with opening up to someone, of the vulnerability that came with love.

My experiences had taught me both the beauty and the pain of relationships, and while I longed for companionship, I was no longer willing to compromise who I was. I wanted someone who could embrace every part of me, without reservation or fear. Until I found that person, I was content to be alone, building a life that was both fulfilling and authentically mine.

The meeting sealed the deal. By the end of my final semester at Yale, I had accepted an offer from Whitaker, Hargrove & Crane. It felt surreal. A highly competitive salary, a generous signing bonus, and a promise that I'd be fast-tracked to work on major cases—a dream offer, really, and one unheard of for new associates. But along with that promise came sky-high expectations. The pressure was daunting, and I knew I had to be at my very best.

Before I could start that new chapter, there was one final challenge: the New York State Bar Exam. The mere thought of it had haunted me for months. Everyone said it was grueling, testing not just my knowledge but also my mental endurance. So, I buried myself in bar prep, drowning in study sessions and practice tests. The weight of expectation pressed down on me—not just from the firm, but from myself. After everything I'd fought for, I couldn't let myself stumble now.

Exam day finally arrived, and I remember standing in the exam hall in lower Manhattan, surrounded by hundreds of aspiring lawyers, each one just as tense and focused as I was. For two days, I poured my heart and soul into those questions, writing about contracts, constitutional law, and criminal procedures until my hand was cramped and my brain felt like it might melt. When it was over, I left the building exhausted yet cautiously hopeful, a tiny flicker of pride beginning to burn in my chest.

The wait for the results was excruciating. I threw myself into anything that could keep me distracted: dinners with friends, weekend hikes to clear my head, and quiet hours spent in my favorite library corners. Then, finally, the results came in—I had passed. Not just passed, but excelled. My scores placed me among the top performers. It was a triumph, a validation of everything I'd fought for, and I let myself savor the moment.

My first day at Whitaker, Hargrove & Crane was a whirlwind of adrenaline and excitement. Walking into the towering glass skyscraper in midtown Manhattan, dressed in my best-tailored navy-blue suit, I felt the magnitude of what I was stepping into. The marble floors gleamed, and the air crackled with the energy of high-stakes deals and corporate ambition. The firm was intimidating, but I moved through the lobby with confidence, my head held high.

As a junior associate in the finance law division, I was thrown straight into the fire. Instead of filing papers or fetching coffee, I was placed on a team handling a massive corporate merger between two global banks. The stakes couldn't have been higher. Under the guidance of Amanda Liu, a senior partner whose strategic brilliance was legendary, I learned the intricacies of corporate governance and financial regulations. It was a trial by fire, but I thrived. Twelve-hour days became the norm, and weekends blurred into work, but the challenge was exhilarating. The office became my new battleground, and I fought each day with the resilience that had carried me through high school and Yale.

My colleagues were a mixed bag. Some were kind and curious, others competitive and cutthroat. Whispers about my intersex identity occasionally rippled through the office, but I held my ground. I never hid who I was, and that authenticity earned me both admiration and respect. The questions and curiosity were handled with grace, just as I'd learned to do with everything else life had thrown at me.

Despite the relentless pace, there were rewards. Lavish client dinners at some of New York's finest restaurants, mingling with executives who shaped markets—it was a world of power and privilege, and I found myself right in the middle of it. Standing in rooms where the future of companies was decided, I realized that I had come so far. This was only the beginning, but I was exactly where I was meant to be.

Finding my own place in Manhattan was the next step toward independence. After countless viewings, I found the perfect one-bedroom apartment in Tribeca, a blend of sophistication and charm. High ceilings, floor-to-ceiling windows overlooking the Hudson River, and a minimalist design that felt luxurious but not overdone. It was my sanctuary, a reflection of the life I had fought so hard to build.

Decorating the space became a labor of love. A plush navy velvet sofa, silk throw pillows, and abstract artwork from local galleries gave the space warmth. The kitchen, with its marble countertops and high-end appliances, became my quiet place in the mornings, where I'd make avocado toast and espresso before diving into the chaos of work. My bedroom was my escape, with soft lavender walls, Egyptian cotton sheets, and a framed photo of my family reminding me of where I came from.

I stood tall at 5 feet 10 inches, with long, straight black hair that fell past my shoulders and baby blue eyes that seemed to see through everything. My body was a testament to my journey, a blend of curves and strength, with C-cup breasts and a 10-inch penis that I had come to embrace with confidence. My anatomy was complex, but it made me uniquely me, a blend of masculine and feminine that defied labels and celebrated authenticity.

My relationships had been just as complex. High school brought Ian, my first love and greatest betrayal. I trusted him, and he shattered that trust, leaving me with scars that took years to heal. Yale brought Jonathan, a brilliant math student who showed me kindness and respect. We loved deeply but parted ways when our futures pulled us in different directions, and though it hurt, we remain good friends.

Then there was Maria. Fiery, passionate Maria came into my life like a whirlwind after I started at the firm. We had a beautiful, all-too-brief romance, full of spontaneity and laughter. But her Catholic upbringing clashed with the reality of my identity, and in the end, love wasn't enough. Since then, there's been nothing. Zilch. Nil. Zero. Work has become my distraction, my lover, my everything.

Sometimes, I wonder if I'll ever find someone who can accept all of me. But until then, I'm building a life that is strong, fulfilling, and authentically mine.

Chapter 2. Life after work.

It was a typical Friday evening in Soho, the kind where the energy buzzed, and the streets felt alive with possibilities. I'd just wrapped up a grueling week at Whitaker, Hargrove & Crane, and the thought of spending the night in a dimly lit bar with a good cocktail felt like the only remedy for the stress that had been building. So, there I was, perched at the end of the bar, swirling an Old Fashioned, when she walked in.

Sabrina Hilton. The name didn't mean anything to me then, but I'd never forget the way she commanded attention the moment she stepped into the room. She was stunning, a blonde with sharp, elegant features and black eyes that seemed to know too many secrets. She was maybe five-foot-six, but she carried herself like someone who was used to being in control. I'd later learn that she was the CEO of a small pharmaceutical company, someone who had just made waves with a revolutionary pill for dementia—though whether it was meant to cure or simply alleviate symptoms, I never quite understood. What I did understand, even in those first few moments, was that she was someone who knew what she wanted.

She made her way over to the bar and, to my surprise, took the stool next to mine. A playful smile curved her lips as she asked, "Rough week?" I must've looked as drained as I felt. We struck up a conversation that started simple—work, favorite bars in Soho, the agony of long hours—but before long, it drifted into deeper territory. Her intelligence was dazzling, her wit razor-sharp, and I found myself caught up in the easy flow of our exchange.

Somewhere between our third and fourth drinks, I decided to tell her the truth. It had always been a risk, especially with someone I barely knew. "Gender-speaking," I said, leaning in, "I'm a bit complicated." Her reaction was something I'll never forget. Her eyes widened, and for a brief, heart-stopping moment, I thought she'd walk away. But then she stayed, curiosity flickering across her features. We continued talking late into the night, and before I knew it, we were checking into a nearby hotel.

Inside, the lobby was quiet, the receptionist glancing up briefly before returning to her book. I led Sabrina to the elevator, pressing the button for the top floor. As we ascended, the tension between us grew palpable, electric.

The elevator doors slid open, revealing a plush, dimly lit hallway. I found the room and unlocked the door, ushering Sabrina inside. The room was luxurious, with a large bed dominating the center, surrounded by rich drapes and elegant furniture.

I closed the door behind us and turned to face Sabrina, her eyes dark with desire. "Are you ready for this?"

Sabrina swallowed hard, her mouth dry. "Absolutely."

I stepped closer, my hands resting lightly on Sabrina's hips. "Good."

We began to undress each other slowly, savoring every touch, every brush of skin against skin. I unzipped Sabrina's dress, letting it fall to the floor in a pool of red fabric. Sabrina shivered as my fingers moved to the clasp of her bra, deftly releasing it and letting it join the growing pile of clothes.

My hands roamed over Sabrina's naked torso, her thumbs brushing the sensitive flesh of her breasts. Sabrina gasped, her nipples hardening under the gentle attention. I bent her head, capturing one dusky peak between her lips, suckling gently.

Sabrina moaned, her hands gliding up my sides to cup my full breasts. "You feel amazing," she breathed, her fingers tracing the outline of my lace-covered cock through the fabric of her panties.

I hummed in agreement, releasing Sabrina's nipple and moving down to her stomach. I knelt in front of Sabrina, my hands reaching behind her to undo the clasps of her stockings and suspender belt. Sabrina lifted one foot then the other, letting me strip off the silky garments until she stood completely bare before me.

My hands trailed down Sabrina's thighs, my fingers dipping between her legs to stroke her wet, swollen folds. Sabrina shuddered, her knees weakening as my touch sent waves of pleasure coursing through her body.

"You're so wet," I murmured, my fingers slipping easily into Sabrina's slick heat. "Do you like this?"

Sabrina nodded, her eyes fluttering closed as she leaned back against the bed. "Yes, please..."

I grinned wickedly, my fingers curling inside Sabrina, exploring every inch of her pulsing flesh. I added a third finger, stretching Sabrina deliciously, my thumb rubbing circles over her clit.

Sabrina's breath came in shallow gasps, her body arching into my touch. "More," she begged, her voice raw with need.

I obliged, slipping a fourth finger inside Sabrina, my touch becoming more frantic. Sabrina cried out, her orgasm building rapidly, cresting like a tidal wave.

"Fuck, Isabella..." Sabrina's voice broke, her body trembling as she rode the edge of climax.

I leaned forward, my tongue darting out to taste Sabrina's juices. The flavor was intoxicating, driving my passion higher. I switched my focus to Sabrina's clit, sucking and nibbling with expert precision.

Sabrina's world exploded, her body convulsing as she came hard, her cries filling the room. I continued to lap at her, ensuring Sabrina's orgasm stretched on and on.

Finally, spent, Sabrina collapsed onto the bed, her chest heaving. I rose, my desire burning fiercely. I stripped off my remaining clothes, revealing my impressive cock and beautifully shaped vagina.

Sabrina watched, awe and lust mingling in her gaze. "My God, Isabella... you're perfect."

I knelt beside Sabrina, her cock standing proudly erect. "Your turn," I said.

Sabrina didn't hesitate. She wrapped her lips around the massive head of my cock, her throat stretching to accommodate the girth. I groaned, my hands threading through Sabrina's hair as I guided her deeper.

"Take it all, baby," I urged.

Sabrina obeyed, her throat working diligently as she took my entire length. My hips thrust rhythmically, fucking Sabrina's mouth with abandon. Sabrina gagged slightly, the sensation both overwhelming and exhilarating.

After several minutes, I pulled back. "Enough foreplay. I want to be inside you."

Sabrina nodded eagerly, her pussy still throbbing from the earlier stimulation. I positioned myself between Sabrina's legs, my cock poised at the entrance to her wet, welcoming hole.

I think my breath quickened as I slid my 10-inch cock into Sabrina's wet, welcoming pussy. Sabrina moaned deeply, her body arching to take in every inch of my thick length. The room was filled with the sounds of our labored breathing and the slick, rhythmic schlicking of flesh against flesh.

"Oh, yes," Sabrina gasped, her fingers digging into my back. "So deep... fuck me, Isabella."

I obliged, my hips moving with a steady rhythm, each thrust pushing my cock deeper into Sabrina's core. I could feel the heat and tightness of Sabrina's pussy gripping my shaft, pulling me in further with each movement. Sabrina's inner walls clenched and released around me, milking me for every drop of pleasure.

My eyes locked onto Sabrina's, seeing the wanton desire reflected there. I gripped Sabrina's hips tightly, guiding her movements, driving my cock harder and faster into the willing body beneath me. The bed creaked under our combined weight, the springs protesting lightly as we rocked together.

Sabrina's nails raked down my back, leaving trails of fire in their wake. She threw her head back, her blonde hair cascading over the pillows like a golden waterfall. Her moans grew louder, mingling with the sound of their bodies colliding, creating a symphony of lust.

"Yes, Isabella! Fuck me harder!" Sabrina demanded, her voice breaking with passion.

I complied, increasing the intensity of my thrusts. I could feel the pressure building in my lower abdomen, the familiar tightening of my muscles signaling my impending climax. But I wanted to savor this moment, to draw out the pleasure as long as possible.

"You feel so good, Sabrina," I said with desire. "I can't get enough of you."

Sabrina's eyes fluttered open, her gaze locking onto mine once more. "Don't stop... I need this... I need you."

My heart swelled with affection for the woman beneath me. I leaned down, capturing Sabrina's lips in a searing kiss. Our tongues danced together, sharing the heat and intensity of our coupling. The taste of Sabrina was intoxicating, a mixture of sweat, arousal, and pure, unadulterated desire.

Breaking the kiss, I pulled out of Sabrina's pussy with a wet pop. Sabrina whimpered in protest, her body aching for more of my touch.

"Turn over," I commanded with authority.

Sabrina obeyed without question, eagerly flipping onto her stomach. She reached back, spreading her cheeks wide, presenting herself to me.

I positioned myself behind Sabrina, my hands caressing the smooth, pale globes of her ass. I lined up my throbbing cock with Sabrina's tight, puckered hole. With a slow, deliberate motion, I began to push inside.

Sabrina groaned, her body tensing as I breached her anal passage. The sensation was different from before, tighter and more intense. I took my time, allowing Sabrina to adjust to the intrusion. Gradually, I sank deeper, until my hips were pressed firmly against Sabrina's ass.

"God, you're so tight," I said in Sabrina's ear.

Sabrina nodded, unable to speak through the overwhelming sensations. She clenched her muscles around my cock, trying to relax and enjoy the feeling of being filled so completely.

I began to move, my thrusts slow and deliberate. Each stroke pushed my cock deeper into Sabrina's ass, stretching her further than she had ever been stretched before. The friction was exquisite, the tightness of Sabrina's ass creating a delicious pressure against my sensitive shaft.

Sabrina's moans grew louder, her body trembling with pleasure. She reached back, grabbing hold of my thighs for support. The sensations were overwhelming, a torrent of pleasure that threatened to drown her.

"Isabella... I can't... I can't take much more," Sabrina panted, her voice shaky with exertion.

I leaned forward, my chest pressing against Sabrina's back. "You can do it, baby. Just let go... let yourself feel everything."

Sabrina did as she was told, releasing the tension in her body. She allowed herself to be carried away by the waves of pleasure crashing over her. The sensation of my cock sliding in and out of her ass was almost too much to bear, but she welcomed it, craving the release that was just out of reach.

My pace quickened, my thrusts becoming more desperate. I could feel my orgasm building, the pressure in my abdomen growing unbearable. I needed to come, needed to release all the pent-up desire that had been simmering within me.

"Sabrina... I'm so close," I groaned.

Sabrina nodded, understanding what I needed. She reached back, grasping my cock with one hand. She used her grip to guide my thrusts, helping me find the perfect rhythm.

With a final, powerful thrust, I buried my cock deep inside Sabrina's ass. I held still for a moment, savoring the sensation of being so completely enveloped. Then, with a shout, I ejaculated, my body convulsing with the force of my orgasm.

Sabrina felt my cum filling her, the warmth spreading through her insides. It pushed her over the edge, sending her spiraling into her climax. Her body shook violently, her pussy clenching around nothing as she came.

I collapsed on top of Sabrina, both of us panting heavily. For a moment, neither spoke, simply enjoying the afterglow of our shared ecstasy.

Finally, I pulled out of Sabrina, my cock slipping free with a wet pop. I rolled onto my back, exhausted but content. "That was amazing," I said. I was fully satisfied.

Sabrina turned to face her, her eyes sparkling with happiness. "It was," she agreed, leaning in for a gentle kiss.

As we lay entwined on the bed, I felt a new wave of desire begin to rise within me. I looked at Sabrina, my mind already picturing the next act of our mutual pleasure.

"What do you want to do now?" I asked.

Sabrina smirked, her eyes twinkling with mischief. "I think... I think we should try something a little dirtier."

Before I could respond, Sabrina leaned down and took my softening cock into her mouth. She sucked gently, tasting the mingled flavors of their sex on my skin.

"God... that feels so good," I whispered, closing my eyes and savoring the sensation.

Sabrina continued to suck, her tongue swirling around my shaft. I could feel the hardness returning to the once-soft member, the stiffness growing with each passing second.

"Enough teasing," I said finally, pulling Sabrina off my cock. "I need you again... properly."

Sabrina grinned, climbing on top of me. She positioned herself over my cock, aligning it with her wet, waiting pussy. With a slow, steady motion, she lowered herself down, taking the full length inside her once more.

I groaned, my hands resting on Sabrina's hips. "Fuck, Sabrina... you feel so good."

Sabrina began to ride my cock, her movements slow and deliberate. She wanted to savor every moment, every sensation, drawing out the pleasure as long as possible.

My hands traveled up Sabrina's body, cupping her breasts and tweaking her nipples. The added stimulation sent shivers down Sabrina's spine, her movements growing quicker and more urgent.

"Touch yourself," I commanded her, with a firm voice.

Sabrina obeyed, reaching down to rub her clit with one hand. The dual sensations of my cock inside her and her fingers on her clit were almost too much to bear. She could feel another orgasm building, the tension coiling tighter and tighter within her.

My fingers found Sabrina's ass entrance, slipping inside with ease. She moved in sync with Sabrina's motions, adding to the overwhelming pleasure.

"Come for me, Sabrina," I urged her.

Sabrina couldn't hold back any longer. With a scream of ecstasy, she came, her body convulsing around my cock and my fingers in her ass. The sensation was so intense, that she thought she might black out from the sheer force of it.

I followed soon after, my orgasm washing over me like a tidal wave. I cried out, my body trembling with the force of the release.

As our climaxes subsided, Sabrina collapsed on top of me, both of us breathless and spent, again. They lay there for a moment, simply enjoying the closeness of their entangled bodies.

"Isabella," Sabrina whispered, her voice barely audible. "You're incredible..."

"And you are absolutely amazing, Sabrina."

We kissed once more, the passion between us burning as brightly as ever.

I was asleep and then I groaned as Sabrina's tongue darted around my clit, the sensation sending electric jolts through my body. I could feel myself growing wetter by the second, the juices pooling in my beautifully shaped vagina and dripping down onto Sabrina's face. Sabrina's hands were busy too, one exploring my ass, fingers teasing at the rim of my tight hole, while the other gripped her cock, stroking it with expert precision.

"Fuck, Sabrina," I said, my hips bucking involuntarily. "You're amazing."

Sabrina looked up, a smirk playing on her lips as she continued to lap at my pussy. "You taste incredible," she murmured, her voice muffled by my folds. "I can't get enough of you."

My breath hitched as Sabrina shifted lower, taking the head of my cock into her mouth. The warm, wet suction was almost too much to bear, and I had to bite my lip to stifle a cry. Sabrina took more and more of the 10-inch length, her throat muscles working expertly as she swallowed around the massive shaft. My hand found its way into Sabrina's hair, fingers tangling in the blonde locks as I guided the woman's head with increasing urgency.

"Oh God, Sabrina," I said. "Don't stop. Take it all. I want to feel your throat around me."

Sabrina's eyes locked with mine for a brief moment, filled with determination and desire before she once again engulfed my cock. This time, she managed to take even more, her nose pressing against the soft skin of my pubic mound. The sensation was overwhelming, and my knees trembled as I fought to stay upright.

"I'm... I'm gonna come," I warned her. "If you keep doing that, I'm gonna come."

Sabrina pulled back slightly, her lips sliding off my cock with a wet pop. "Not yet," she panted, her own need evident in her eyes. "I want to feel you inside me first."

With that, Sabrina moved back up the bed, positioning herself so that her glistening pussy hovered just above my waiting cock. I reached up to guide her, the tip of my cock nudging against Sabrina's entrance. Sabrina took a deep breath, her eyes closing as she slowly lowered herself down, inch by agonizing inch.

"Yes," Sabrina whispered, her voice trembling with anticipation. "Yes, like that."

My hands roamed over Sabrina's thighs, feeling the warmth and smoothness of her skin. I could feel every millimeter as my cock slid deeper, stretching Sabrina open, filling her completely. Sabrina's walls tightened around me, gripping my shaft like a vice, and I let out a low groan of pleasure.

"You feel so good," I said. "So fucking good."

Sabrina nodded, her eyes still closed as she adjusted to the sensation of my large cock inside her. Finally, she was fully seated, her hips resting against my pelvis. The feeling was unlike anything she had ever experienced, a mix of fullness and ecstasy that made her head spin.

"God, Isabella," Sabrina breathed, her eyes fluttering open. "Your cock is... it's perfect."

I was pleased by the compliment. "Let's see how perfect it feels when we start moving," I said, my tone playful but filled with intent.

With that, I began to thrust upwards, my hips meeting Sabrina's downward movements with perfect rhythm. The room was filled with the sounds of our bodies slapping together, the wet squelch of flesh on flesh, and the occasional moan or gasp. Sabrina's hands found their way to my breasts, squeezing and kneading the firm mounds as we fucked.

"Harder," Sabrina begged, her voice breaking. "Please, harder."

I complied, picking up the pace until they were both moving with feverish urgency. Sabrina's back arched, her head thrown back as waves of pleasure crashed over her. She could feel her orgasm building, the pressure coiling tighter and tighter in her core.

"I'm close," Sabrina panted, her nails digging into my shoulders. "So close."

I didn't reply, too lost in my pleasure to manage words. Instead, I redoubled my efforts, driving my cock deeper and faster, my release looming on the horizon. Sabrina's walls clenched around her, milking my cock with each thrust, and I knew they were both about to come.

"Sabrina... I'm gonna—" I said, but Sabrina cut me off with a desperate kiss.

Our tongues dueled as our bodies moved together in perfect harmony. Sabrina could feel the tension in my muscles, the strain of holding back, and she ground her hips harder, determined to push us both over the edge.

"Come for me," Sabrina whispered between kisses. "Come inside me, Isabella."

And I did.

The next two days were a whirlwind of passion. We made love like lunatics, our bodies entwined as we shut out the world and lost ourselves in each other. It was raw, exhilarating, and intense in a way that left me breathless. By Monday morning, I was exhausted yet deliriously happy. We exchanged numbers and agreed to call each other, but there were no promises, just the lingering memory of a weekend that had been pure, unfiltered bliss.

I went back to my high-stakes world of corporate law, expecting nothing. So when she called on Thursday to arrange a dinner, my heart skipped a beat. She sounded different, more serious, and mentioned something about the dinner being "for three." Intrigued and a little nervous, I agreed.

Friday night, I found myself sitting at **Le Bernardin**, a three-Michelin-star restaurant in Midtown Manhattan. The ambiance was opulent, the kind of place where the wine flowed as smoothly as the conversation. When Sabrina walked in, she looked effortlessly glamorous, dressed in a sleek black dress that highlighted her perfect figure. But she wasn't alone. Beside her was a man, tall, with sandy brown hair, piercing blue eyes, and an easy charm that made him look like he belonged in a boardroom or on a yacht. This was Christopher Hilton, her husband, and yet another CEO—this time of a tech startup.

The introductions were warm, but the tension crackled under the surface. I had never expected this twist, but as the evening unfolded, the three of us fell into an unexpectedly comfortable rhythm. Christopher was charismatic and intelligent, and the conversation flowed as easily as it had between Sabrina and me. By the time dessert arrived, I had almost forgotten my initial nerves. There was an unspoken understanding developing between us, one that became glaringly obvious when Christopher leaned over and asked if I'd like to join them for the weekend.

I was out of my depth but undeniably curious, so I said yes.

What followed was a weekend that felt like a fever dream. We checked into a penthouse suite at a luxurious hotel, and for two days, we explored each other's bodies with reckless abandon. It was intoxicating, an experience that blurred the lines between fantasy and reality. I had never felt so free, so desired. The three of us fit together in a way that felt almost surreal, and I found myself letting go of inhibitions I didn't even know I had.

I glanced over at Christopher, who was still watching us with a hungry look in his eyes. The penthouse was filled with the scent of our combined arousal, a heady mix of sweat and sex that made my cock twitch. Sabrina's moans were a constant soundtrack, each one driving me closer to the edge.

"Chris, why don't you join us?" I suggested, my voice thick with desire. "There's plenty of room for all of us."

He hesitated for a moment, then nodded, his gaze never leaving Sabrina's glistening body. He moved towards us, his hands already unbuttoning his pants. I watched as he freed his erection, a respectable size that would complement mine perfectly.

Sabrina gasped as Chris positioned himself behind her, aligning his cock with her entrance. She looked over her shoulder at him, her eyes wide with anticipation. "Yes, please," she breathed, her voice trembling with excitement.

Chris didn't waste any time. He pressed into her slowly, his thrusts deliberate and deep. I could see the muscles in his arms tense as he worked, his face a mask of concentration. Sabrina whimpered, her fingers digging into my shoulders as she struggled to stay upright.

"Fuck, you feel so good," Chris growled, his voice strained. "So tight."

I leaned down to kiss Sabrina, my tongue slipping between her lips as she took my cock deeper into her mouth. Our bodies moved together in a synchronized rhythm, each thrust of Chris's hips matched by my downward pressure. The sound of our flesh meeting filled the room, along with the wet slapping of Sabrina's eager mouth.

"Keep going," I whispered against her lips. "Take it all, baby."

Sabrina nodded, her eyes fluttering closed as she focused on the task at hand. I could feel her throat working around my cock, her muscles contracting in response to every movement. It was almost too much to bear, the sensation of being swallowed whole by her talented mouth while her husband pounded into her from behind.

I reached down to cup Sabrina's breasts, squeezing her nipples between my fingers. She arched her back, pressing into my touch as Chris's pace quickened. The room was filled with the sounds of our breaths, hot and ragged, mingling with the occasional moan or gasp.

"Isabella," Chris called out, his voice breaking. "I need... I need more."

I pulled out of Sabrina's mouth, letting my cock rest against her cheek as I considered his request. My asshole clenched at the thought of Chris inside me, but I knew I couldn't deny him. Not now, not when we were all so close to the edge.

"On your knees," I instructed, turning to face him. "But be gentle. This is my first time."

Chris nodded; his eyes dark with lust. He knelt behind me, positioning his cock at my entrance. I bit my lip, bracing myself as he pushed forward. The feeling was intense and overwhelming, but not unpleasant. His cock slid into me inch by inch, filling me in a way that felt both foreign and exhilarating.

"Oh God," I groaned, leaning forward to rest my forehead on the bed. "That's... that's good."

Chris began to move, slowly and steadily at first, giving me time to adjust. His hands gripped my hips, pulling me back onto his cock with each thrust. The sensation of being filled from both ends was almost too much to handle, my body trembling with the effort of staying upright.

Sabrina crawled up beside me, her eyes shining with mischief. She reached out to stroke my cock, her fingers circling the tip before sliding down to the base. The added stimulation sent a jolt of pleasure through my body, making me arch into her touch.

"You like that?" she purred, leaning in to kiss my neck. "Feeling Chris inside you?"

I could only nod, my breath coming in short gasps. The combination of Sabrina's touch and Chris's relentless thrusts was pushing me closer to the edge. I could feel my orgasm building, a slow simmer that threatened to boil over at any moment.

"Faster," I managed to whisper, my voice barely above a whisper. "Please, faster."

Chris obliged, picking up the pace until his thrusts were almost frantic. I could feel his balls slapping against my skin with each movement, the sound echoing in the room. Sabrina continued to stroke my cock, her fingers moving with expert precision as she coaxed me closer to the edge.

"Almost there," she murmured, her lips brushing against my ear. "Just a little more."

I close my eyes as Christopher's cock pushes deeper into me, his hands gripping my hips with a firm yet gentle force. The sensation is overwhelming, a blend of intense pleasure and the primal urge to surrender to him completely. I can feel every ridge and vein on his shaft as it moves inside me, each thrust sending waves of heat through my body. My moans escape into the room, mingling with Sabrina's eager breaths as she positions herself in front of me.

Sabrina's eyes lock onto mine, her emerald green irises shimmering with desire. She lowers herself onto my cock, her movements deliberate and controlled, her lips curling into a mischievous smile as she impales herself on my 10-inch dick. The sensation is electric, a powerful surge that shoots through me from the base of my spine to the tips of my fingers and toes. I watch in awe as her body takes me in, inch by glorious inch until I am fully sheathed inside her.

"Oh, God," Sabrina gasps, her voice trembling with the intensity of the moment. "Isabella, you feel so... so good."

Her pussy grips my cock tightly, the walls contracting around me in rhythmic pulses that match the rhythm of Christopher's thrusts. I can feel the warm, slick friction of her inner muscles working against me, coaxing every ounce of pleasure from my body. The smell of sex fills the room, a heady mix of sweat and arousal that only heightens the sense of urgency between us.

Christopher's thrusts become more urgent, his pace quickening as he finds his rhythm. His grunts echo in the room, a deep, guttural sound that speaks to the raw power of his desire. He leans forward, his chest pressing against my back as he whispers in my ear, "You like that, Isabella? You like feeling us fucking you?"

I nod, unable to form words as the sensations overwhelm me. My hands grip the sheets beneath me, my nails digging into the fabric as I try to anchor myself to the bed. Sabrina's hands find my breasts, her fingers teasing my nipples, adding another layer of stimulation to the already intense experience.

"Fuck, yes," Sabrina groans, her hips moving in sync with Christopher's thrusts. "We're all connected, aren't we? All of us, sharing this... this incredible connection."

Her words resonate within me, filling me with a profound sense of connection and unity. I can feel the energy between us, a tangible force that binds our bodies together in a dance of lust and love. The room seems to fade away, leaving just the three of us, lost in the exquisite torment of our shared pleasure.

Sabrina's movements become wilder, her body bouncing on my cock with a reckless abandon that mirrors the desperation in her voice. She looks up at me, her eyes filled with a mixture of ecstasy and vulnerability. "Isabella, please... make me come. Make me come hard."

Hearing her plea, I tighten my muscles, my cock throbbing inside her as I focus on hitting every sensitive spot within her pussy. Christopher matches my tempo, his thrusts becoming more erratic as he nears his climax. The sound of our bodies slapping together fills the air, a chaotic symphony of flesh on flesh that only serves to drive us further toward the edge.

"I'm so close," Christopher murmurs, his voice thick with exertion. "So fucking close."

Sabrina's breath hitches, her body tensing as she feels the first waves of her orgasm building. Her pussy clenches around my cock, the contractions rippling down my length and igniting a fire within me. I can feel the pressure building, the need to release coiling tighter and tighter within my gut.

"Come for us, Sabrina," I whisper, my voice shaking with the force of my desire. "Let go and come for us."

With a cry that echoes through the room, Sabrina arches her back, her entire body convulsing as she reaches the peak of her orgasm. Her pussy milks my cock with a ferocity that leaves me breathless, the sensation so intense that I can barely think. My vision blurs, the edges of reality fraying as I feel myself teetering on the brink.

Christopher roars behind me, his body shuddering as he spills himself inside me. The warmth of his release mingles with the throbbing pulse of my impending climax, creating a perfect storm of ecstasy that pulls me under. My world narrows to the point where Sabrina and Christopher meet through me, the three of us fused in an explosion of pure, unadulterated pleasure.

"Yes, Isabella," Sabrina moans, her voice a distant echo as my mind blanks out in the face of overwhelming sensation. "Yes, yes, yes..."

I ejaculated at the same time, my sperm filling her pussy.

After a thirty-minute break, Sabina was eager to go again.

Sabrina's eyes fluttered open, her breath coming in short, ragged gasps. The bed beneath her was a tangled mess of sheets and limbs, the air thick with the scent of sweat, musk, and sex. She could feel Christopher's cock sliding inside her anus, his thrusts slow and deliberate now, but no less powerful. My cock nestled deep within her other channel, the sensation overwhelming yet incredibly intoxicating.

"Isabella," Sabrina moaned, her voice husky and filled with desire. "I can't... I can't believe how good this feels."

I smiled at her dark eyes gleaming with satisfaction. "Believe it, darling. You deserve every bit of pleasure we can give you."

Christopher growled low in his throat, his hips snapping forward with renewed vigor. "Let's not stop just yet, ladies. There's still so much more to explore."

Sabrina whimpered, her body trembling as she felt another wave of pleasure building within her. "Yes, please... don't stop..."

I leaned down, my lips brushing against Sabrina's ear. "Close your eyes, sweetheart. Let yourself go."

Sabrina obeyed; her eyelids fluttering shut as she surrendered to the sensations coursing through her body. She could feel the weight of both me and Christopher on either side of her, our bodies pressing against hers in a symphony of flesh and bone. The sound of their breathing, their grunts of effort, and the wet smacking of skin against skin filled her ears, creating a soundtrack to her ecstasy.

Christopher's hands gripped her hips tightly, his nails digging into her flesh as he drove his cock deeper into her. "Fuck, Sabrina... you feel amazing," he panted, his voice strained with exertion.

My hands roamed over Sabrina's body, her fingers tracing patterns along her curves before settling on her nipples. She gave them a gentle pinch, eliciting a sharp intake of breath from Sabrina. "You like that, don't you?" Isabella purred, her voice dripping with sensuality.

"Yes," Sabrina gasped, her chest heaving with each breath. "Please, more..."

I obliged, my fingers working in tandem with Christopher's thrusts, pushing Sabrina ever closer to the edge. She could feel her arousal mounting, her slick folds clenching around my cock as she teetered on the brink of orgasm.

Christopher's hand moved to cup her mound, his fingers slipping easily between her swollen lips. He found her clit, rubbing it in circles as he continued to pound into her. "Come for us, Sabrina," he commanded, his voice firm and authoritative.

Sabrina's mind went blank, her entire being focused on the sensations flooding her body. She could feel her orgasm building, the tension coiling tighter and tighter within her. With one final, desperate cry, she shattered, her body convulsing around the cocks buried inside her.

Christopher and I followed suit, our orgasms crashing over them in waves. I cried out, my hips jerking as I came, my cock pulsing inside Sabrina. Christopher roared, his release filling Sabrina even as his thrusts became erratic and wild.

The three of us lay intertwined, our bodies slick with sweat and spent from their efforts. Sabrina felt a sense of overwhelming contentment wash over her, the afterglow of their shared climax lingering in the air.

"That was... incredible," Sabrina murmured, her voice soft and dreamlike.

I smiled, my fingers playing idly with Sabrina's hair. "Agreed. But I think there's still more we can explore."

Christopher raised an eyebrow, his blue eyes twinkling with mischief. "Oh? And what did you have in mind, Isabella?"

My smile widened, a predatory glint in my eyes. "How about we try something new? Something... different."

Sabrina felt a thrill of anticipation race through her veins. "Different? What do you mean?"

I leaned in close, my lips inches from Sabrina's. "I want to try double vaginal penetration. Both of us inside you at the same time."

Sabrina's breath caught in her throat, her heart pounding with excitement. "Are you sure you can... fit?"

I grinned, my confidence unwavering. "We'll make it work. Trust me."

Christopher's cock twitched inside her, a clear sign of his interest. "Count me in. Let's see if we can push the boundaries even further."

Sabrina nodded slowly, her resolve firming. "Okay. Let's do it."

I kissed her softly, a trail of kisses leading down her neck and chest. "Good girl. Now, let's get ready."

Christopher withdrew from Sabrina, sitting back on his heels as I positioned myself between Sabrina's legs. Sabrina watched, her breath hitching as she realized what was about to happen.

I guided my cock to Sabrina's entrance, pressing gently until the head slipped inside. Sabrina groaned, her muscles relaxing to accommodate the intrusion.

"Now, Chris," I said, my voice steady and calm.

Christopher positioned himself behind her, his cock pressing against Sabrina's other entrance. Sabrina bit her lip, her body tensing as they prepared to enter her simultaneously.

"Ready?" Christopher asked, his voice laced with urgency.

Sabrina nodded; her eyes squeezed shut. "Do it."

With one smooth motion, both me and Christopher pushed forward, forcing our way into Sabrina's tight pussy. Sabrina's back arched, a strangled cry escaping her lips as the stretch overwhelmed her senses.

"Easy, baby," I whispered, my fingers stroking Sabrina's thigh reassuringly. "Just breathe."

Sabrina took deep, steadying breaths, her body gradually adjusting to the feeling of being doubly penetrated. She could feel both cocks moving inside her, the sensation intense and almost too much to bear.

Christopher's hands settled on her hips, his grip firm but gentle. "How does that feel, Sabrina?"

Sabrina's voice was barely a whisper. "It's... it's amazing. Keep going."

I began to move, my thrusts slow and deliberate. Christopher matched my rhythm, our movements synchronized as they worked to maximize Sabrina's pleasure

Sabrina's head fell back, her breath coming in short gasps as she rode the wave of sensation. She could feel her arousal building again, the pressure inside her growing with each thrust.

"So close," she moaned, her body trembling with need.

"Then come for us," I urged her. "Let go, Sabrina."

With a cry that seemed to come from deep within her soul, Sabrina's orgasm exploded, her body convulsing around the cocks buried inside her. Me and Christopher erupted in response, our orgasms mingling with hers as they reached the peak together.

The room was filled with the sounds of our passion, the air electric with energy as we clung to each other, bodies trembling with the force of their release.

As the last tremors subsided, Sabrina felt a deep sense of fulfillment, her body sated and satisfied. She looked up at me and Christopher, our faces glowing with triumph and affection.

"That was... incredible," she whispered, her voice filled with wonder.

I smiled, my fingers tracing lazy circles on Sabrina's thigh. "There's still more we can explore if you're willing."

Sabrina's eyes sparkled with anticipation. "I'm willing. Lead the way, Isabella."

"We are both going to fuck you in the ass. Your first double anal. Is that ok, darling?" I asked.

"Yes, but please be gentle," Sabrina answered with certain trepidation in her voice.

I leaned in close to Sabrina, my breath warm against her ear as I whispered, "Are you ready, darling? This is going to be intense." She nodded, her eyes wide but filled with anticipation. I could see the mix of trepidation and excitement in her gaze, and it only made me more eager to guide her through this new experience.

Christopher positioned himself behind Sabrina, his hands gripping her hips firmly. I knelt in front of her, my large cock already hard and throbbing with desire. I reached out, gently parting her ass cheeks, revealing the tight pucker of her anus. My fingers traced the delicate line of her spine, down to where our bodies would soon meet.

"Just relax," I murmured, placing a soft kiss on her lower back. "We'll go slow."

Sabrina took a deep breath, her body trembling slightly. Christopher and I exchanged a glance, silently communicating our intention to be as gentle as possible. I pressed the tip of my cock against her opening, feeling the warmth radiating from her body. Slowly, I began to push, inch by agonizing inch, until the head of my cock breached her barrier. Sabrina gasped, her nails digging into the sheets beneath her, but she didn't pull away.

Christopher followed suit, positioning himself at her other entrance. I could see the tension in his muscles as he prepared to enter her, his cock slick with lube. With a slow, deliberate motion, he pushed forward, the head of his cock meeting mine inside her anal passage. Sabrina cried out, a sound that was equal parts pain and pleasure, as the two of us filled her.

The sensation was overwhelming. The way our cocks rubbed against each other inside her, the heads meeting and pressing together, created a friction that was both intense and deliciously stimulating. I could feel Christopher's rhythm, matching my thrust for thrust, as we moved in unison within her. Each thrust sent shockwaves of pleasure through my body, making my cock throb even harder.

Sabrina's moans grew louder, her body arching under the dual pressure of our cocks. Her fingers clawed at the bedspread, her breaths coming in short, sharp gasps. I could see the strain in her face, but also the unmistakable signs of her pleasure—her flushed cheeks, her tightly closed eyes, the way her body trembled with each thrust.

"You're doing so well, darling," I whispered, my voice strained with effort. "Feel how good it feels... feel how full you are..."

Christopher grunted, his thrusts becoming more forceful as he found his rhythm. "God, Sabrina... your ass is incredible..."

I watched as Sabrina's face contorted with pleasure, her mouth opening slightly as if to speak, but no words came out. Instead, a series of guttural noises escaped her lips, mingling with our heavy breathing and the wet sounds of our cocks moving within her.

The room was filled with the scent of sex, thick and heavy, mingling with the faint aroma of sweat and the sweet smell of lube. The air seemed to vibrate with the intensity of our movements, the bed creaking beneath us as we continued our relentless rhythm.

As we neared our climax, I felt a surge of urgency build within me. My cock pulsed against Christopher's; the pressure was nearly unbearable. Sabrina's body tightened around us, her inner anal muscles clenching in what I knew was the prelude to her orgasm.

"Christopher... get her mouth," I panted, my voice barely above a whisper.

He nodded, understanding immediately. He withdrew briefly, causing Sabrina to whimper with need, before guiding her head down to my cock. Her lips parted, wrapping around the sensitive head just as I felt the first spurt of my orgasm building. My ejaculation filled her mouth to the brim.

"Don't swallow," Chris demanded.

Christopher followed suit, his release coming swiftly as he thrust into her mouth again and again. His cum joined mine, filling her to overflowing, the combined pressure pushing her over the edge. Sabrina's body convulsed, her orgasm crashing over her like a tidal wave. She screamed around Chris' cock, her throat vibrating with the force of her climax.

Her cries were muffled, her mouth full of our cocks as she continued to come, her body shuddering with the intensity of her pleasure. I could feel her tongue flicking against the underside of my shaft, adding another layer of sensation to the already overwhelming experience.

As our orgasms subsided, I slowly withdrew from her mouth, the sensation leaving a hollow ache in its wake. Christopher did the same, and we both collapsed beside her, our breathing ragged and our bodies slick with sweat.

Sabrina's mouth remained open, her tongue working to clean the remnants of our cum from around her mouth. I couldn't help but smile, as we proceeded to a three-way kiss, swapping the sperm from her mouth to mine and then Christopher's.

Finally, satisfied, she was released from our embrace and looked up at me, her eyes filled with wonder. "That was... incredible," she whispered, her voice trembling with emotion.

By Monday morning, I woke up to an empty bed, the sunlight streaming through the curtains. Sabrina and Christopher had already left, but on the bedside table, there was an envelope. Inside was $5,000 in crisp bills. My heart sank, and I felt a flush of anger and humiliation. Was that all this had been to them? I called Sabrina, my voice shaking. "I'm not a hooker," I said, my words tumbling out.

Her laughter on the other end of the line was soft but not unkind. "Isabella," she said, "you're not a hooker. You're our girlfriend. You're entitled to some gifts." Her words left me stunned, but they also shut me up. In a world where everything was transactional, this was something different—something I wasn't sure I knew how to navigate.

The weeks that followed were a mixture of confusion, excitement, and a sense of unpredictability that left me feeling like I was living in two parallel worlds. On one hand, I had the structured, high-pressure environment of Whitaker, Hargrove & Crane, where every day was a battle of intellect and resilience. On the other, there was the world of Sabrina and Christopher Hilton, a place where boundaries blurred and the rules I'd lived by no longer seemed to apply.

The envelope of money had initially thrown me off balance, but Sabrina's explanation—that I was their "girlfriend," not just some fling—intrigued me more than I cared to admit. Her words echoed in my mind, mixing with the thrill of our weekend together. The idea of being part of something so unconventional both terrified and excited me.

It didn't take long for the Hiltons to reach out again. Sabrina called one evening while I was still at the office, poring over the details of a multimillion-dollar merger. Her voice, smooth and commanding, instantly pulled me out of my work-induced daze. "We'd like to see you again," she said, her tone leaving no room for doubt. Something was intoxicating about how direct she was, and before I knew it, I was rearranging my schedule to make time for them.

That Friday evening, I found myself stepping into the Hiltons' world once more, this time at their penthouse apartment on the Upper West Side. The place was breathtaking, a testament to their wealth and impeccable taste. Floor-to-ceiling windows offered a panoramic view of the city, and the space was filled with an understated elegance: sleek furniture, abstract art, and subtle touches that screamed sophistication without ever feeling ostentatious.

Sabrina greeted me with a glass of champagne and a kiss that left me breathless. Christopher appeared moments later, his smile easy and warm. The dynamic between the three of us was still new, still raw, but there was an undeniable chemistry. We spent the evening talking, laughing, and eating a gourmet meal prepared by their private chef. The conversation flowed effortlessly, and I found myself charmed by Christopher's wit and Sabrina's sharp intelligence.

As the night unfolded, the three of us moved from the dining room to the plush living room, the city lights shimmering outside like a million scattered diamonds. Sabrina leaned in close, her lips brushing against my ear as she whispered, "Are you ready for more?" I felt my heart race, the anticipation electrifying. We moved to the master bedroom, and once again, I found myself swept up in the whirlwind that was Sabrina and Christopher. Our bodies tangled together, exploring and connecting in ways that felt both exhilarating and intimate.

What surprised me most was the sense of genuine connection I felt, something deeper than just physical attraction. The Hiltons were attentive, making sure I felt wanted and safe, and that gave me a sense of security I hadn't expected. They were both powerful, confident people, but with me, there was a vulnerability that seemed to surface, as though they, too, were exploring uncharted territory.

As the weeks went on, our relationship continued to evolve. It wasn't just about sex, though that was certainly a part of it. The three of us would have dinners together, attend art exhibitions, or simply spend evenings curled up on the sofa, debating politics or discussing the latest scientific breakthroughs. Sabrina would talk passionately about her work in pharmaceuticals, her eyes lighting up as she described the new dementia pill and the potential it held. Christopher, in turn, would share stories from the tech world, painting vivid pictures of the future he was helping to build.

There were moments of tenderness I hadn't anticipated. Christopher would brush a strand of hair out of my face, his touch gentle and almost reverent. Sabrina would run her fingers down my spine, tracing patterns as we lay together, her voice soft as she asked me about my day. It was strange and wonderful, this feeling of being cared for by two people who were so different yet so perfectly in sync.

But it wasn't without complications. The first time I saw Sabrina and Christopher together, alone and intimate, a pang of jealousy took me by surprise. It was in the way they looked at each other, a connection that had been built over years of marriage, and I couldn't help but wonder if I was just an interlude, a temporary thrill. Yet, every time those doubts crept in, one or both of them would do something to reassure me, to make me feel that I was a valued part of whatever we had created together.

Balancing this unconventional relationship with my demanding career was a challenge. There were days when I barely had time to breathe between meetings and casework, let alone think about romantic entanglements. Yet, the Hiltons became a source of comfort. On especially stressful days, a text from Christopher—"Thinking of you"—or a voice message from Sabrina, playful and full of affection, was enough to make the stress melt away, if only for a moment.

One weekend, we escaped the chaos of the city and drove up to their lake house in the Catskills. It was a place I could never have imagined myself being, surrounded by nature and luxury in equal measure. We spent our days hiking and our nights wrapped in each other's arms, the world feeling miles away. It was there, by the firelight, that Sabrina admitted she had never felt this way about another person before. "We're not just using you, you know," she said, her voice vulnerable in a way I hadn't heard before. "This... this is real for us." Christopher nodded, his eyes sincere, and I knew then that whatever this was, it was something worth holding onto.

Still, there was always an undercurrent of uncertainty. My world and theirs were so different, and I couldn't help but wonder how long this could last. Were we destined to crash and burn, or could this truly become a lasting part of my life? And then there was the money. Sabrina and Christopher were generous, showering me with gifts I wasn't sure how to accept. Expensive jewelry, trips to exclusive resorts, and once, a new designer handbag that must have cost more than my rent. They insisted these were just tokens of their affection, but I still struggled to reconcile their wealth with my fiercely independent nature.

I wasn't used to being spoiled, to having people treat me as though I was something precious. Yet, with them, I found myself slowly letting go of my defenses. Maybe it was the way they both listened when I spoke, genuinely interested in what I had to say, or the way they treated me like an equal partner in our little triangle. Whatever it was, it felt real, and for the first time in a long time, I allowed myself to believe that I deserved to be happy.

The next part of my journey with the Hiltons took a turn I hadn't anticipated, one that pulled me deeper into their world. I knew from the start that Sabrina and Christopher were unconventional, but nothing quite prepared me for the revelation that came on a quiet Tuesday evening.

Sabrina and I were sharing a bottle of red wine at her favorite spot in the East Village, a quaint wine bar with low lighting and an intimate atmosphere. We'd been talking about work, about a documentary we'd both watched, when she casually mentioned, "By the way, Christopher and I are hosting a little dinner on Friday. For six." She tilted her head, watching for my reaction.

"Six?" I repeated, setting my glass down. My heart thumped as I tried to mask my confusion.

She smiled, that playful, teasing smile I'd come to know so well. "We have some friends we'd like you to meet," she said. "We're... open about certain things, and we'd love for you to join us." Her tone was casual, but her eyes were searching for mine, waiting to see if I'd be put off.

The implication wasn't lost on me. They were swingers. Big-time swingers. I took a moment to process, my mind racing. This was new territory, even for someone like me, who had never shied away from exploring her sexuality. "Okay," I finally said, my voice steady despite the whirlwind in my chest. "I'm in."

Friday arrived, and I found myself in Little Italy, walking into a charming Italian restaurant with Sabrina and Christopher by my side. The place had an old-world charm, with brick walls and a warm, inviting ambiance. The scent of garlic and fresh pasta filled the air, and I had to remind myself to breathe.

We were led to a private dining room where the other guests were already waiting. Martin and Eleonora, a striking couple in their late thirties, greeted us warmly. Martin had a rugged handsomeness, with salt-and-pepper hair and a disarming smile, while Eleonora looked like she had stepped out of a Renaissance painting, all dark curls and elegant curves. Then there was Justin, their "boyfriend," a young, athletic man with a mischievous grin and a sparkle in his eyes.

Introductions were made, and before long, the conversation flowed as smoothly as the wine. I was surprised at how easily everyone clicked. We talked about everything from travel to books to the complexities of modern relationships. It was like a gathering of old friends, though an undercurrent of anticipation buzzed beneath the surface, a shared secret that made the air feel electric.

By the time dessert arrived, I had started to relax. Sabrina's hand found mine under the table, a silent reassurance that I wasn't alone in this. Christopher leaned over and whispered something to Martin, who laughed and nodded. It was clear that everyone knew where the night was headed, and yet, the unfolding was slow and deliberate, like a dance we were all learning together.

After dinner, we walked back to the Hiltons' penthouse. The elevator ride up was filled with nervous laughter and lingering glances. When we stepped into the apartment, the city lights sprawled out below us, sparkling like a blanket of stars. Sabrina closed the door behind us, and for a moment, there was only the sound of our breathing.

Christopher took the lead, his voice smooth and confident. "Make yourselves comfortable," he said, gesturing toward the plush living room. We settled into the space, and the atmosphere shifted, growing more charged with each passing second.

Sabrina moved toward me; her eyes locked onto mine. "Are you ready?" she whispered, her fingers brushing my cheek. I nodded, my heart pounding in my chest, but it was a thrill I couldn't resist.

What happened next was a blur of passion and connection, an experience unlike anything I had ever imagined. Clothes fell away, and the six of us moved together like an intricate, sensual dance. Martin's hands were rough but gentle, tracing lines along my skin. Eleonora's lips found mine, soft and searching, as we explored each other with a hunger that felt both primal and tender. Justin was playful between Isabella and Christopher, his laughter infectious as he tangled himself into the mix, making every touch and caress feel like a celebration of freedom.

Justin was impressive, his dick being just as big as mine and as he laid down on the sofa, Isabella and Christopher were sucking, in turns his massive cock, both deep-throating him. They have been very familiar with each other.

On the other sofa, an identical image was happening, with me in the middle of Eleonora and Martin, With Martin licking my pussy while Eleonora was deep-throating my huge erection. I was indeed super excited with all this arrangement and especially that my pussy was seeing finally some action. The other weekend, when fucking Chris and Sab, Chris did indeed fucked me in my pussy, but considering that Sab was supposed to be the center of attention, we both concentrated our attention on one task, to make her happy and cum as many times as humanly possible.

This time, no one was the center of attention, especially when cameras were involved. We all agreed to film this amateur porno session, as we are admittedly both exhibitionists and voyeurs. Four static cameras were placed on tripods getting every possible angle, and all transmitted to the four massive screens in the living room. It was an unbelievable scenario, electric and exciting at the same time, seeing ourselves on the screen.

It was time for a little change, as Eleonora joined Justin and Chris on their sofa, while Sab positioned herself on top of me, with her cunt straight on my mouth, opening her pussy wide open with her fingers for me to reach as deep as possible. Martin's dick was just average, which is no criticism, but it was big enough to satisfy any woman, comfortably. He was now fucking me, his dick in and out of my pussy, in a very slow rhythmic movement, while I was happily lapping Sab's pussy juices.

On the other sofa, Eleonora was riding, facing up Justin's massive cock. His dick was in and out of her pussy, her legs wide open for Chris to lick their fuck. His tongue was pushing between Justin's dick and Ely's vaginal walls. He was covered with their fuck juices. Not soon after that, he pushed his dick alongside Justin's into her cunt. She was in a delirium trance of pleasure, coming at every few seconds interval.

Meanwhile, on my sofa, Sab was now vaginally impaled into my dick. Martin was happy to fuck me while I fucked her, but then he discovered heaven, two pussies in front of him so he was alternating between double vaginally penetrating Sab, or just penetrating me. But then he discovered that our asses were free as well, so he started alternating, ass-vagina-ass-vagina, and so on.

Martin's dick pressed into me, his rhythm steady and insistent. I could feel Sabrina's wet heat clenching around my shaft as she rode me, her breaths coming in quick gasps. The room was alive with the sounds of our desires, a symphony of moans and slaps and whispered encouragements. The screens above us played our every move back in real-time, the digital mirrors making the experience even more surreal.

"Isabella, come here," Justin called out, his voice rough with desire. He had Ely pinned beneath him, their bodies a tangle of limbs and passion. "Need you to join us."

I didn't need to be asked twice. I slipped out from under Sabrina, who pouted but quickly found solace in Martin's eager touch. I moved to the other sofa, positioning myself behind Ely. Her eyes were half-lidded, pupils blown wide with pleasure, and she whimpered as I lined myself up with her entrance.

"Ready?" I murmured, teasing her with just the tip of my cock.

"Fuck yes," she managed, arching her back to meet me.

I pushed in slowly, savoring the tightness of her body and welcoming me. Justin's cock was already deep inside her, and as I thrust in beside him, we created a perfect rhythm. His hips snapped against hers, driving both of us deeper. I could see the strain on her face, the way her lips parted to let out a breathless moan.

"Christ, this is amazing," Justin groaned, his hand finding mine on Ely's hip.

"Mmm, feels so good," Ely agreed, her nails digging into my forearm.

Across the room, Sabrina was now sandwiched between Chris and Martin, their cocks moving in tandem inside her. She looked over at us, a wicked grin spreading across her face. "You guys look like you're having fun over there."

"Join us if you want," I offered, pulling out slightly to give her space.

Sabrina hesitated for only a moment before slipping off the sofa and straddling Ely's face. She lowered herself down, her pussy meeting Ely's searching tongue. Ely gasped around her, the sensation clearly overwhelming.

"Oh fuck," Sabrina breathed, her thighs trembling as Ely's skilled tongue worked its magic.

The room was a haze of intertwined bodies now, each of us feeding off the others' energy. I felt a rush of adrenaline as I watched the screens, seeing myself buried deep inside Ely while Sabrina writhed above her. It was intoxicating, the way our actions were immortalized in pixels, replayed for us to watch as we fucked.

"Switch it up," Chris suggested, his voice hoarse. "Let's change partners again."

We all nodded, the hunger for new sensations driving us. Ely slid off Justin's cock with a sigh, and I backed away, giving them space. Sabrina rose from Ely's face, her hair wild and her skin slick with sweat.

"My turn," she declared, stepping over to me. She knelt down, taking my cock into her mouth with practiced ease. Her lips wrapped around me, hot and soft, and I let out a groan as she began to suckle me deeply.

Martin and Chris shifted positions, Chris now behind Eleonora while Martin took his place in front of her. They fucked her together, their movements synchronized as they pumped into her from both ends.

"God, you're so tight," Martin grunted, his fingers digging into her hips.

"Feels incredible," Eleonora replied, her head lolling back as she took them both.

I watched them for a moment, the sight of two cocks sliding in and out of Eleonora's body too enticing to ignore. My cock twitched in Sabrina's mouth, her tongue swirling around the sensitive head.

"Sabrina, stop," I said, pulling her off me. "I want to try something else."

She looked up at me, curiosity sparkling in her eyes. "What do you have in mind?"

"Help me get on top of Eleonora," I said, already moving toward the sofa where she lay spread-eagle.

Sabrina followed, her hands guiding me as I positioned myself above Eleonora. I aligned my cock with her entrance, feeling the warmth of her body inviting me in. With a slow, deliberate thrust, I entered her, the tightness nearly unbearable.

"Oh fuck," Eleonora cried out, her nails raking down my back.

I started to move, my hips slapping against hers in a steady rhythm. Sabrina stayed close, her hands roaming over my back and shoulders, adding pressure where needed.

"You like that?" I asked, leaning down to nip at Eleonora's earlobe.

"Yes," she gasped, her legs wrapping around my waist. "So much."

From the corner of my eye, I saw Chris and Martin watching us, their dicks hard and ready. They exchanged a look before Chris stepped forward, positioning himself behind me. I glanced back, raising an eyebrow in question.

"Mind if I join?" he asked, his cock nudging against my ass.

"Not at all," I replied, shifting slightly to allow him entry.

Chris pushed in, his cock sliding into my ass with surprising ease. I groaned the dual sensations of Eleonora's pussy and Chris's cock sending waves of pleasure through me. We moved together, a seamless trio, each thrust timed perfectly.

"Fuck, this is incredible," Chris muttered, his hands gripping my hips tightly.

Eleonora's cries grew louder, her body trembling beneath us. "Don't stop, please don't stop."

Sabrina watched, her breath hitching as she took in the scene. "My turn," she announced suddenly, pushing Martin aside.

She straddled Eleonora's face, lowering herself down so that her pussy hovered inches from Eleonora's mouth. Eleonora eagerly licked at her, her tongue darting out to taste Sabrina's juices.

"Yes, oh god," Sabrina moaned, her body shaking as she rode Eleonora's face.

I could feel my climax building, the pressure mounting with every thrust. Chris's cock rubbed against my prostate, driving me closer and closer to the edge.

"Almost there," I panted, my thrusts growing erratic.

"Me too," Chris agreed, his grip tightening.

Eleonora's eyes fluttered closed, her body tensing as she came hard beneath us. Her orgasm seemed to push us both over the brink and with one final, powerful thrust, I released deep inside her. Chris followed suit, filling my ass with his cum.

"Oh fuck," Sabrina cried out, her orgasm hitting her as she ground against Eleonora's face.

We collapsed onto the sofa, our bodies spent and satisfied. For a moment, there was only the sound of our heavy breathing, the afterglow enveloping us like a warm blanket.

"That was... amazing," Eleonora whispered, her voice shaky.

"Agreed," I replied, still catching my breath.

But the night was far from over. Across the room, Martin and Justin were already gearing up for another round, their dicks hardening again as they watched us. Sabrina caught my eye, a mischievous glint in her gaze.

"Think you're up for more?" she asked, already moving to straddle Eleonora again.

"Always," I replied, my cock twitching in response.

As I settled back into position, ready to dive into the next wave of pleasure, I couldn't help but glance at the screens. Our actions were being recorded, captured forever in the digital realm. And as I thrust into Eleonora once more, I knew this was just the beginning of our exhibitionist escapades.

I could feel the heat radiating from Sabrina's body as she straddled me, her wetness enveloping my throbbing erection. Martin's hands guided his dick into my pussy, alternating thrusts with his rhythm, maintaining a steady pace that sent waves of pleasure crashing over me. I glanced at the screens to see our images on display, the visual stimulation adding an extra layer of excitement to the experience.

"Let's mix it up," Justin's voice broke through the haze of sensation. "Ely, switch with Isabella. Let's see how you handle double penetration too."

Eleonora grinned, her eyes sparkling with mischief as she dismounted Justin and Chris. I took her place, my legs spreading wide as I positioned myself above Justin's massive cock. Chris moved behind me, his hands gripping my hips as he aligned himself for entry. The initial stretch was intense, but the pleasure quickly overtook any discomfort, and I found myself riding Justin while Chris pounded into me from behind.

Martin and Sabrina watched for a moment before deciding to join in. They moved to the adjacent sofa, where Sabrina positioned herself on all fours, offering her ass and pussy to Martin and Christopher. Martin alternated between penetrating Sabrina's pussy and ass, while Christopher focused on her clit, their combined efforts driving her wild.

I could hear Sabrina's moans mingling with Eleonora's cries of pleasure, the sounds echoing through the room like a symphony of lust. My breaths came in short gasps as I adjusted to the overwhelming sensation of being filled by both Justin and Chris. The cameras captured every angle, the screens showing our entangled bodies in vivid detail.

"Fuck, Isabella, you're so tight," Chris muttered, his fingers digging into my flesh as he pushed deeper. "I can't believe how good this feels."

"Don't hold back," I panted, meeting Justin's gaze. "I want to feel everything."

Eleonora, watching us from her position on the floor, crawled closer, her hand reaching out to stroke my thigh. Her touch was electric, sending ripples of pleasure through me. She leaned in, her lips brushing against mine in a soft kiss that tasted like salt and desire.

"You're doing great," she whispered, her breath hot against my ear. "Keep going, keep feeling."

The encouragement spurred me on, and I rode Justin harder, my movements becoming more frantic. Chris matched my pace, his thrusts deep and relentless. The sensations were overwhelming, building to a crescendo that I could feel in every fiber of my being.

Meanwhile, Sabrina had reached her peak, her body writhing under the dual assault of Martin and Christopher. Her cries echoed through the room, a testament to the intensity of her orgasm. Martin pulled back, his cum spilling onto Sabrina's back, while Christopher continued to tease her clit, prolonging her pleasure.

"Your turn," Martin said, moving to stand beside me. He stroked his still-hard cock, watching as I continued to ride Justin and Chris. "Show me how much you can take."

I nodded, my focus narrowing to the task at hand. Martin positioned himself behind me, aiming for my ass as Chris withdrew momentarily. The initial stretch was intense, but Martin's expert touch eased the discomfort, and soon I was fully impaled on both ends. The sensation was intoxicating, each thrust bringing me closer to the edge.

Justin's hands gripped my hips, guiding my movements as I bounced on his cock. Chris re-entered my pussy, filling me once again. The triple penetration was too much to bear, and I could feel my orgasm building rapidly.

"Cum for me," Justin growled, his voice low and commanding. "Let go, Isabella."

The command was all it took. A wave of ecstasy crashed over me, and I screamed as my orgasm tore through me. My body convulsed, muscles tightening around the invading cocks as I came hard. The sensation was indescribable, a mixture of pain and pleasure that left me breathless.

As my climax subsided, I felt Martin pull out, his cum dripping from my ass. Chris withdrew next, leaving me splayed and exposed on top of Justin. Eleonora moved to kneel beside me, her hand gently tracing the lines of my body.

"You were amazing," she murmured, her lips pressing a soft kiss to my forehead. "Such a beautiful release."

Sabrina joined us, her cheeks flushed with post-orgasmic bliss. "That was incredible," she breathed, her eyes wide with awe. "I've never felt anything like it."

Martin and Christopher moved to stand beside Eleonora and Sabrina, their cocks still hard and ready for more. The room hummed with sexual energy, the air thick with the scent of sweat and musk.

"One more round?" Martin suggested, his voice laced with anticipation. "Let's finish this off right."

"Definitely," Justin agreed, his grin widening. "But let's make it even more interesting. How about some oral?"

The suggestion hung in the air, the tension palpable. Sabrina and Eleonora exchanged a glance, both nodding in agreement.

"Let's do it," Eleonora said, her voice firm. "But let's make it count."

With that, the group shifted positions once again, the energy in the room shifting and blending as we prepared for the final act.

I could feel the intensity of the moment building as Martin and I continued to alternate between Sabrina's pussy and ass. Her moans grew louder, echoing through the room, mingling with the sounds of Eleonora and Justin's pleasure on the other sofa. The cameras captured every detail, projecting our entangled bodies onto the screens with vivid clarity.

Eleonora's eyes met mine, her breath coming in ragged gasps as she rode Justin's thick cock, Chris's tongue still darting between them. She gave me a wink, her cheeks flushed with arousal, and I knew it was time for another permutation.

"Let's switch," I panted, pulling myself away from Sabrina's quivering body. Martin looked at me, his eyes dark with desire, but he nodded and gently withdrew from her.

I moved swiftly to the other sofa, positioning myself behind Eleonora. Justin groaned as I reached around to stroke his shaft, my fingers gliding over his slick, pulsating length. "Fuck her hard, Isabella," he whispered, his voice hoarse with need.

With a grunt, I slid my cock inside Eleonora's wet, welcoming pussy, feeling the tight warmth envelope me. She gasped, arching her back as I thrust into her, Justin's dick driving deep inside her from the front. Chris's tongue never missed a beat, lapping at their combined juices, creating a symphony of slurping and moaning that filled the room.

On the other sofa, Sabrina was now being pleasured by both Christopher and Martin. Christopher had positioned himself above her, his dick plunging into her mouth as Martin alternated between her pussy and ass. Sabrina's eyes were half-closed, her lips wrapped around Christopher's shaft, her hips rising to meet Martin's thrusts.

The scene was electric, each movement synchronized with the others, creating a sensual ballet of bodies and desires. The cameras recorded everything, capturing the raw, unfiltered passion that flowed between us.

"Faster," Eleonora begged, her voice breaking with urgency. "Yes, right there!"

I complied, increasing my pace, my hips slamming into hers with relentless force. Justin matched my rhythm, his hands gripping her thighs tightly. Chris's tongue flicked faster, his pleasure evident in his groans.

Eleonora's orgasm hit like a tidal wave, her body convulsing around our intertwined shafts. She screamed, the sound sharp and piercing, as she came, her pussy pulsing with intense contractions.

Seeing her climax triggered something primal in me, and I felt my release building. "Justin, I'm close," I warned, my voice strained.

"Me too," he grunted, his face contorted with effort.

We both reached the precipice at the same moment and with one final, powerful thrust, we erupted inside Eleonora. My cum spurted into her depths, mixing with Justin's, filling her up completely.

As the waves of pleasure subsided, I pulled out and quickly moved back to Sabrina, who was still being pleasured by Christopher and Martin. She looked up at me, her eyes glazed with satisfaction, and I knelt beside her.

"Time to finish this," I murmured, leaning in to share a passionate kiss with her. Our tongues danced together, tasting the mingled flavors of sweat and sex.

Martin finally pulled out of her, and Christopher shifted position, bringing his glistening cock to Sabrina's waiting mouth. "Suck it," he commanded softly, and she obeyed, taking him deep into her throat.

At the same time, I positioned myself so that my dick was hovering just above Eleonora's open mouth. She eagerly took me in, her lips wrapping around my sensitive tip as she sucked greedily.

The room was filled with the sounds of our shared pleasure, the cameras capturing every intimate moment. We were lost in a haze of lust and connection, our bodies and souls intertwined.

As Sabrina swallowed Christopher's load, I felt my second orgasm approaching. Eleonora's skilled mouth brought me to the brink, and with a shuddering groan, I came again, flooding her mouth with my essence.

We all collapsed into a heap on the floor, tangled together in a mess of limbs and satisfied smiles. The cameras continued to roll, recording the aftermath of our explosive encounter.

"That was incredible," Sabrina breathed, her voice soft and content.

"Agreed," Eleonora said, wiping a bit of cum from the corner of her mouth. "But I think we could use a shower."

Grinning, we all agreed and slowly untangled ourselves from each other. The penthouse had a massive shower room, and we made our way there, still naked and glowing with the afterglow of our shared experience.

The water was warm and soothing as it cascaded over us, washing away the sweat and cum from our skin. We laughed and joked, our conversation light and playful, as we soaped each other up and rinsed off.

Eventually, we dried off and got dressed, moving back to the living room where we poured glasses of wine and settled in. The screens were still showing the recorded footage of our encounter, and we watched it with a mix of pride and amusement.

As we sipped our drinks, the conversation turned to plans and potential encounters. "I have a few friends who might be interested in joining us next time," Martin said, his eyes gleaming with excitement.

"That would be awesome," Sabrina replied, her voice filled with anticipation. "The more, the merrier."

We continued to discuss our fantasies and desires, the night stretching out before us like an endless canvas of possibility. And as we talked, I couldn't help but feel a thrill of excitement at the thought of what adventures awaited us in the future.

Sabrina and Christopher remained the anchors in this swirling storm of desire, their presence grounding me even as everything else spun out of control. I found myself surrendering to the moment, to the intensity of six bodies coming together in a way that was both chaotic and beautiful. There was no jealousy, no sense of competition—only an overwhelming sense of unity, of being a part of something larger than myself.

Hours passed, and the night melted into the morning, the city lights eventually giving way to the soft glow of dawn. We lay together in a tangle of limbs and silk sheets, exhausted yet content. The adrenaline slowly faded, leaving behind a sense of surreal wonder. I couldn't believe what I had just experienced, couldn't believe how right it had felt, even if it defied every expectation I'd ever had about love, sex, and connection.

Later that morning, as I pulled myself from the bed to find some water, I stumbled across Christopher in the kitchen. He was making coffee, his hair tousled and his smile easy. "Good morning," he said, handing me a mug. "How are you feeling?"

I took a sip, letting the warmth spread through me. "Surprisingly good," I admitted, and he laughed, the sound low and full of understanding.

Sabrina joined us a moment later, wrapping an arm around my waist. "You were incredible," she murmured, her lips brushing against my neck. The affection felt genuine, and I realized that this world they'd invited me into, as complicated and unconventional as it was, might be exactly what I needed.

But I also knew that this wasn't just about pleasure. It was about trust, vulnerability, and the willingness to explore the unknown. And as I stood there in the warmth of their embrace, I wondered where this path would lead me next—and whether I was ready for all the complications that came with it.

Waking up that Sunday morning, the golden sunlight filtering through the Hiltons' floor-to-ceiling windows, I felt a curious mix of exhilaration and contentment. My body ached pleasantly from the night before, a vivid reminder of everything we had shared. Laughter, touches, kisses—all of it was still fresh in my mind, lingering like a heady, intoxicating perfume. I stretched lazily, savoring the warmth of the silk sheets and the view of the city sprawled out below.

I had just begun gathering my things—dressing quietly, careful not to wake anyone still dozing in the suite—when I reached into my handbag to grab my phone and found an envelope. My heart skipped a beat, and I felt a flush of disbelief as I pulled it out, my fingers trembling slightly. Inside were crisp $100 bills, neatly bundled. I did a quick count. $6,000.

I stood there for a moment, the envelope heavy in my hands, as confusion, embarrassment, and anger washed over me. It was one thing to receive a gift from the Hiltons. It was another to find this, a seemingly impersonal wad of cash as if I were being paid for services rendered. Memories of the first time this had happened—when Sabrina had left $5,000 on the bedside table—came rushing back, and I could feel my pulse quicken with the familiar sting of being misjudged, of feeling commodified.

It didn't take me long to find Sabrina. She was in the kitchen, dressed in a simple silk robe, hair tousled but looking effortlessly elegant. She was pouring herself a cup of coffee, and when she saw me, her face lit up with that dazzling smile. But she immediately noticed my expression and her brow furrowed slightly.

"Is everything okay?" she asked, her voice warm but laced with concern.

I took a deep breath, holding up the envelope. "I found this in my bag," I said, trying to keep my voice steady. "$6,000. Care to explain?"

Sabrina's eyes softened, and she set her coffee down, leaning casually against the counter. "Ah," she said, as if understanding everything at once. "It's a gift. From us—and Martin and Eleonora."

I felt my frustration bubble to the surface. "So, what does that mean?" I demanded, my voice rising slightly. "Am I their girlfriend too? Is that how this works now?"

Sabrina didn't miss a beat. Her response was simple, spoken with a confidence that only she could exude. "Of course you are."

And just like that, the wind was knocked out of my sails. Again. Her words were so matter-of-fact, so unashamedly sincere, that they shut me up on the spot. I stood there, grappling with what she had said, trying to process this unconventional world I had stepped into. To them, this wasn't about money or transactions. It was about connection, about the way I had become a part of their lives, something more significant than I had dared to expect.

Sabrina walked over to me, placing a gentle hand on my arm. "Isabella," she said softly, "this isn't about payment. It's about appreciation. You're important to us—to all of us. This is just a way of making sure you know that. A way of showing that you matter."

Her explanation made sense in a way I couldn't quite argue with, even if it left me conflicted. I had always prided myself on my independence, on never needing or relying on anyone's generosity. And yet, here I was, being cared for, cherished even, by people who wanted me in their lives and weren't shy about expressing it.

I swallowed, the tension in my chest easing slightly. "I don't know how to feel about all of this," I admitted.

Sabrina's expression softened even further. "You don't have to decide how to feel right now," she said. "Just know that we care about you. Deeply."

We stood there for a moment, the silence between us heavy but not uncomfortable. I looked down at the envelope in my hands and let out a shaky laugh. "You know how to complicate things, don't you?" I said.

Sabrina chuckled, her laughter warm and genuine. "That's what makes life interesting."

That morning, as I left the penthouse and stepped back into the bustling world of Manhattan, I couldn't stop thinking about what Sabrina had said. The lines between romance, friendship, and this peculiar arrangement were blurring in ways that felt both thrilling and terrifying. I had been pulled into something bigger than myself, something I hadn't anticipated but was undeniably curious to explore.

And as complicated as it was, I couldn't help but feel that maybe, just maybe, I was exactly where I was supposed to be.

Two weeks after that unforgettable night with Martin, Eleonora, Sabrina, and Christopher, I found myself standing on the brink of a career-defining opportunity. The week had been a blur of late nights and endless paperwork at Whitaker, Hargrove & Crane, but everything changed when I received two life-altering phone calls.

The first was from Martin O'Callahan. He was the owner of O'Callahan Logistics, the second-largest logistics company in New York, and his wife, Eleonora, ran O'Callahan Construction, the fourth-largest construction company in the city. They were titans in their industries, and I had come to know them as both clients of pleasure and partners in adventure. Martin's voice over the phone was as smooth and self-assured as ever. "Isabella," he said, "Eleonora and I have been discussing our legal representation, and we'd like you to become our lawyer. We want you to handle everything."

I nearly dropped my phone. My heart was pounding as I processed his words. Securing the business of two of New York's most powerful companies would be a game-changer—not just for me but for the entire firm. "I'd be honored," I managed to say, my voice steadier than I felt. "I promise I won't let you down."

Before I could even catch my breath from that conversation, my phone buzzed again. This time, it was Sabrina Hilton, the gorgeous, enigmatic CEO of a small but rapidly growing pharmaceutical company. She and her husband, Christopher, a tech startup wizard, had become integral parts of my life, both personally and now, it seemed, professionally. Sabrina got straight to the point. "Christopher and I have a proposition for you," she said. "We'd like you to handle our legal needs as well. It makes sense to keep everything in the family, doesn't it?"

The sheer magnitude of what she was offering nearly floored me. With Sabrina's pharmaceutical empire and Christopher's tech firm, I would be bringing four major companies into the fold at Whitaker, Hargrove & Crane: logistics, construction, tech, and pharma. It was the kind of business that most junior associates could only dream about landing, and here it was, being offered to me on a silver platter.

The next day, I found myself in the firm's grand conference room, pitching my proposal to the senior partners. Gregory Whitaker, the firm's founding partner, sat at the head of the table, his steely gaze fixed on me. The room was filled with the most powerful lawyers in the city, and the weight of their expectations pressed down on me like a physical force. But I was ready.

"Martin and Eleonora O'Callahan, along with Sabrina and Christopher Hilton, are prepared to bring their businesses to our firm," I began, my voice steady. "That includes one of the largest logistics companies in New York, a major construction firm, an innovative pharmaceutical company, and a tech startup that's on the verge of a breakthrough. This isn't just about expanding our client list—it's about solidifying our reputation as the go-to firm for industry leaders."

There was a moment of silence, then Gregory leaned back in his chair, his expression unreadable. "This is an extraordinary opportunity," he said slowly. "Are you sure you're prepared to handle the responsibility?"

I met his gaze without flinching. "Absolutely," I replied. "I've built relationships with these clients based on trust and mutual respect. I'm ready to take this on."

After a tense pause, he nodded. "Then you have our full support."

The days that followed were a whirlwind of activity. My calendar filled up with meetings, contract negotiations, and high-stakes strategy sessions. I had gone from being a junior associate to a rising star at the firm, and the pressure was immense. But I thrived on it, driven by the knowledge that I was carving out a place for myself in a world that had never come easily to me.

Working with the O'Callaghan was exhilarating. Martin's logistics empire was a labyrinth of supply chains and international trade agreements, and I had to immerse myself in the intricacies of shipping regulations and corporate partnerships. Eleonora, with her construction projects, required a different set of skills. Her work involved navigating zoning laws, labor contracts, and city permits, and every decision had millions of dollars riding on it. The O'Callaghan was demanding but fair, and I found myself learning more in a few weeks than I had in years of law school.

The Hiltons were another story. Sabrina's pharmaceutical company was on the cutting edge of research, and handling her legal needs meant delving into FDA regulations, patent law, and corporate governance. Christopher, with his tech firm, introduced me to a world of venture capital, intellectual property disputes, and data privacy concerns. The complexity was dizzying, but I loved every minute of it.

My life became a balancing act, a high-wire performance between my professional obligations and my deeply personal connections to the people I now represented. Sabrina and Christopher continued to be a source of comfort and excitement, our time together a thrilling escape from the stress of work. The lines between lawyer, lover, and friend blurred in ways I never could have anticipated, but I wouldn't have had it any other way.

Martin and Eleonora, too, occupied a special place in my world. They were more than just clients. Eleonora would call me late at night, her voice warm and reassuring, to check in and see how I was holding up. Martin would invite me out for drinks, sharing stories about the challenges of running a family business and offering advice that was equal parts practical and inspiring. We had built something that transcended the usual boundaries of business, a relationship that was as deeply rooted in trust as it was in mutual ambition.

But there were complications. My colleagues at Whitaker, Hargrove & Crane were starting to notice the rapid ascent of my career, and with that came envy and whispers. Some speculated about how I had managed to land such high-profile clients, and I knew some were eager to see me stumble. The pressure was suffocating at times, but I had been through worse. I had survived the cruelty of high school, the grueling demands of Yale, and the struggle to find my place in a world that often didn't know how to accept me. I could handle this.

One evening, after another long day at the office, I found myself at the Hiltons' penthouse, sipping a glass of wine and unwinding from the week's chaos. Sabrina sat beside me, her fingers brushing mine in a gentle, intimate gesture. "You've been amazing," she said, her voice full of admiration. "Taking on all of this—us, the work, the chaos. You make it look easy."

I laughed, though the sound was wearier than anything else. "It's far from easy," I admitted. "But it's worth it."

Christopher joined us, wrapping an arm around my shoulders. "You know we're proud of you, right?" he said, his voice warm and genuine. "We're all in this together."

And in that moment, I realized just how much my world had changed. I was no longer just Isabella, the intersex teenager who had once struggled to find her place. I was now Isabella, a powerful, respected lawyer on the rise, with a chosen family that believed in me and a career that was finally becoming everything I had dreamed of.

But I also knew that this was only the beginning. The path ahead was full of uncertainty, and the stakes would only get higher. Yet, for the first time, I felt ready to face whatever came next, knowing that I had built something that was mine—a life of complexity, ambition, and a love that defied convention.

.............................To Be Continued

Page |

Also by Malcom Adrian Highgate

Gangbang wife
Gangbang Wife Part 1
Gangbang Wife Part 2

My Intersex Life
Both And Neither Part 1

Swingers Stories
Swingers Stories Part 1
Swingers Stories Part 2
Swingers Stories Part 3

Thirteen Inches
Thirteen Inches Part 1
Thirteen Inches Part 2

www.ingramcontent.com/pod-product-compliance
Lightning Source LLC
Chambersburg PA
CBHW061617130726
47996CB00003B/1007